a dog called
HOUDINI

a dog called Houdini

C. Everard Palmer

Cover by
Susan Gardos

Scholastic Canada Ltd.

Scholastic Canada Ltd.
175 Hillmount Road, Markham, Ontario, Canada L6C 1Z7

Scholastic Inc.
555 Broadway, New York NY 10012, USA

Scholastic Australia Pty Limited
PO Box 579, Gosford, NSW 2250, Australia

Ashton Scholastic Ltd.
Private Bag 94407, Greenmount, Auckland, New Zealand

Scholastic Ltd.
Villiers House, Clarendon Avenue, Leamington Spa,
Warwickshire CV32 5PR, UK

Canadian Cataloguing in Publication Data

Palmer, C. Everard
  A dog called Houdini

ISBN 0-590-73465-2

1. Dogs - Fiction. I. Wilson, Maurice, 1914-
II. Title.

PR9265.9.P35D6 1992   j813   C91-094186-6

Copyright © 1978 by C. Everard Palmer.
Cover illustration copyright © 1998 by Susan Gardos.
Interior illustrations copyright © 1978 by Maurice Wilson.
This edition published by Scholastic Canada Ltd. by arrangement
with André Deutsch Limited, London. All rights reserved.

7 6 5 4 3   Printed in Canada   8 9/9 0 1 2/0

Contents

*This book is written in memory of Brownie,
the Thunder Bay dog which evaded dog-catchers
for a number of years and which was eventually
poisoned by a person or persons unknown.*

1
Bubba

The old couple who owned Houdini's mother loved dogs. But when she had a litter of five healthy puppies, they realized they could not afford to feed them all. They were relieved when they managed to find good homes for four of the pups.

Then one day a young man and his wife came to the old couple's home. They found a spunky little puppy that yapped bravely at them and boldly nipped their fingers. This one was the old couple's favourite. He was the healthiest, smartest pup in the litter, and they had planned to keep him. But the young man and his wife pleaded for him until the old couple reluctantly gave in. They stood together on the porch of their house and watched the young couple drive off with their fine pup, consoling themselves with the thought that he had found a good home.

But the young man and his wife had lied to the old couple. They did not really care about dogs. They

lived on a lonely road in northern Ontario, and they wanted the pup only as a watchdog for their isolated house. They were often away all night or all weekend, sometimes even for a week at a time, and they would leave the puppy without food or water or even shelter from the cold and rain.

Chained to a tree, the puppy would whimper with cold and loneliness. Day after day he grew thinner and weaker. Then one dark night the rotten leather thong around his neck broke. The chain slithered to the ground and the pup was free.

When Old Man Raith, the trapper, came back from town the next morning he heard crying in the bushes and stopped to see what it was. He picked up the skinny, quivering pup he found crouching there, tucked him inside his shirt, took him home and fed him back to health. Whatever he ate, the pup ate.

Pork and beans. Baked beaver tail. Dried fish, venison, moose. The little dog gobbled it all up.

Soon he was happy, chubby and alert again. He explored the tiny log cabin and chased all the rats away. He lay, head between his paws, in front of the wood stove each evening. He followed Old Man Raith everywhere, never letting him out of his sight.

At first Old Man Raith took the dog in his leather bag when he went to check his traps. The puppy's head stuck out through the top and he looked at his surroundings with the keen eye of an explorer. Soon he was strong enough to accompany Raith on his own short legs, running ahead or dropping back to sniff out interesting trees or clumps of bushes.

The old man and the dog even went to town together, for there was only one thing that the dog feared, and that was being tied up. The first time Old Man Raith had tried to leave him behind while he went to town, the pup, half-grown by this time, went berserk. He threw himself about, nearly tearing the rope in half, then jumped on his hind legs, yelping in despair. Since Old Man Raith didn't know the dog's history, he could not understand this violent reaction. But he was moved by the dog's misery and never tied him up again.

Whenever they went to town to sell furs to the local Hudson Bay store, the pup waited outside. He didn't interfere with the dogs that wandered by and he didn't allow them to interfere with him. He didn't allow them close enough even to smell him, keeping them off with a snarl that showed his white fangs.

He didn't allow people to touch him or pet him either, giving them the same treatment he gave the town dogs. Luckily, he never had to use his teeth. Showing them was enough.

The pup grew stronger and smarter day by day. Old Man Raith worked him as hard as he worked himself, and as the two of them walked the trap lines or ate supper in the tiny cabin together, the old trapper talked to the young dog as he would to a friend.

He called him Bubba.

Bubba learned everything from Old Man Raith. He learned how to carry loads into town in deer-hide packs strapped to his sides. He learned how to retrieve the ducks that the old man shot each fall. He learned how to track game, how to flush birds from their hiding place, how to run down a rabbit for the old man's dinner. Working side by side, the young dog and the old man lived as one.

Then one day when they were out checking traps in the deep snow, the old man slipped and fell and never got up again. His heart had stopped. Bubba barked at him to get up. But nothing would budge the old man, not even tugs at his sleeve.

A heavy snow began to fall, and yet the old man lay there, face down, his snowshoed legs splayed

awkwardly. Bubba's barks turned into whines as he milled around the trapper in nervous mourning, scraping off the snow as it all but covered the man who had been his only friend.

The snow continued to fall well into the night, and Bubba stayed. He yearned for the warmth of the log cabin but he stayed with the man who had showed him love and kindness. Finally his instinct told him to let the snow be, to let it cover his friend. It was a burial. Retiring to a rock ledge, he watched the white mound grow.

He went back to the cabin at last but he could not get in, and even if he could have, he would have found nothing to eat. Since the dried meat hung high in the rafters, he had to find his own food. He turned to rabbits.

It was a month before a man came by the cabin on a snowmobile. Bubba picked up the sound while it was still a good distance away and knew it was heading for the cabin. He took off in that direction, but the machine got there ahead of him. When he arrived the rider was already standing in front of the door.

"Raith!" he was calling. "Raith!"

Bubba knew him. He had come to the cabin before on his machine and had sat with the old man drinking coffee in front of the stove, laughing and talking. He had seen him in town too. Bubba barked once and the man, Abel Hilkkanen, a retired lumberjack, turn-ed. "Hey, Bubba. Where you bin? Where's Raith? Come here, boy."

He noticed the dog's ribs showing through his matted coat. Something was wrong. He looked back at the cabin, the yard in front. There were no tracks in the snow, no footsteps but his own at the door. The snow was piled in the doorstep. Although he had sunk in the deep snow, somehow it hadn't meant anything to him until now. "Where's Raith, boy?"

Bubba barked again, once, and turned and trotted off.

"Oh, no," Abel said. "Oh, no. Something's hap-pened to Raith." He began to follow the dog.

Bubba stood by the mound and began to scoop the snow away with his paws, whining all the time. Abel joined in with his mittened hands. Old Man Raith was in the same position as he had been when he fell, only now he was frozen stiff. Abel covered him again. That night he came back with help and they took the old man out on a sled.

Bubba followed at a distance but he did not allow anyone to come near him. He attended the funeral too, whining nervously throughout the brief cere-mony. Then, with the old man's body gone, he be-came confused about what to do. He could not stay in town and so returned to the cabin. But there was nothing for him there.

A week later, Abel and a woman — Old Man Raith's daughter — came and emptied the cabin. They tried to coax Bubba to go home with them, but he wouldn't go near them or let them near him. Yet he knew that his home here had come to an end.

After they left, he took one last look at the empty cabin, at the closed door and the boarded-up windows. He barked once, then turned and headed off into the forest.

For three months he lived off rabbits and other small game. But then he found easier meals. Northern Ontario is dotted with summer camps, and Bubba quickly learned that the pets city people brought with them were no match for him. Soon he could snatch a meal from under the nose of another dog and race away into the woods before the owners even saw him.

Once again he filled out and became contented. But when the nights began to get longer, fewer campers came to the area. Finally, in October, Bubba felt hungry for the first time since spring.

He sniffed the cool, crisp air. Perhaps he smelled the chow mein at Yung Foo's. Perhaps the Cosy Cafe was cooking bacon that morning. Whatever the reason, Bubba did not go back to hunting rabbits. Instead, he turned east and headed off down the road to Mayor Frederick's town.

2
The Town

The town sits at the tip of one of the many fingers of Lake Superior. It is in Canadian Shield country, where countless smaller lakes dot limitless green forests, where granite hills rise up to stand guard over a land rich in wildlife. The town itself is just a few hundred metres off the Trans-Canada Highway and is now the home of five thousand people.

In the time of the voyageurs, it was only a landing spot. Here they camped on their long journey and did a little trading with the Indians. But then a Jesuit priest arrived to establish a mission and work among the Indians. A small trading post grew up. Then a sawmill was built, for the surrounding forest was rich in timber. Now the town has grown, as have the other towns in the north, till there are restau-

11

rants, hotels, taxi cabs and gas stations, banks, two grocery stores, schools, churches, an arena and a car dealership.

But the sawmill is still there. It grew with the years and now its salt-shaker stacks stand proudly over the town. Thousands of pieces of lumber zing through its saws each year. Huge logs arrive at the mill on heavy tandem trucks and planks leave on railcars or tractor-trailers.

The town started around the waterside landing of the voyageurs, so this is where the older houses stand. But as it grew, the town spread to the hills overlooking the bay. The Mayor lives in this new part, and from his living room window he can look with pride over the whole town, the town he has managed for eleven years.

Except for the Indians, the people of the town all come from somewhere else. Most of them have fathers or mothers who were Finnish, British or French. They are friendly people. Even with strangers they do not pass by on the sidewalk without speaking or at least nodding hello. When they do stop to talk, they are very interested in the weather.

"Cold enough for you?"

They have many cold days.

"Lovely day, isn't it?"

A lovely day is one when the sun shines, even if the thermometer reads –30°C.

During the long winter months the people play hockey and skate in the town arena or go ice-fishing, skiing and snowmobiling. In the summer the tourists arrive. Everyone takes to the water, and weekends are spent by the lake or in the woods where people relive the old days of wood smoke, outhouses and kerosene lamps, and fish and swim or skim the lakes in high-speed boats.

When fall comes and the trees glitter with brilliant leaves the hunters go to the woods and the forest echoes with the boom of guns. First they hunt the partridges, then deer and moose.

But then the tourists leave, and the people of the town are alone again. They all settle back into their old routines for the long winter. Everyone begins to pay close attention to whatever causes a ripple in the town.

Even the arrival of a strange dog is not to be taken lightly — especially one as remarkable as the dog that people started to notice just shortly after the last tourist left the town in early October.

He was medium-sized and seemed to be part cocker spaniel, part terrier. Whatever he was, he looked like an ordinary mutt. But he was different.

No one knew exactly where he had come from. Someone had seen him around the camps at a nearby lake earlier that summer, and people suspected that a camper had left him behind and gone back to the city.

At first he was just a stray dog. But soon he was "that black-and-white dog." Later he became "that darn dog."

He was seen everywhere, from one end of town to the other. He invaded back yards and snatched the dinners of dogs just as they came to eat them. He chose his victims carefully, leaving the German Shepherds and the St. Bernards alone. But the big dogs that couldn't fight he terrorized, much to the embarrassment of their owners.

Dog owners in town began to talk about him. Their dogs were becoming nervous wrecks. They would stand over their dog burgers at meal times, looking up nervously after each mouthful. That darn dog was unpredictable.

Children began to resent the fact that they had to stand guard in their own back yards while the family pet ate. They began to call the dog a marauder. Even those without dogs began to notice the newcomer.

He didn't much like cats that sunned themselves on porches or fence rails. He raced after them, happy to see them bolt, wide awake and fully active. He didn't like the pigeons that cooed and scrabbled in front of the town hall either. He sent them swarming into the air in a flutter of wings whenever he came upon them. Then he would turn to the old men and women who sat on the benches as if expecting ap-

proval — but his enthusiasm earned him nothing but shouts.

"Leave them birds alone!"

"Git out of here, you darn dog!"

The grandmothers and grandfathers were afraid of this whirlwind, and the dog was confused by them. What were they doing, sitting about on park benches? Why weren't they working? He didn't have much use for relaxation himself, and didn't understand retirement at all.

Even people standing on the sidewalks annoyed him. As they stood chatting, he would barrel out of a lane or from behind a garbage can just to get them moving along. It almost seemed that he was playing a game. But for the people of the town it was unnerving not to be able to stand and talk about the weather without looking nervously over their shoulders for a black-and-white marauder bearing down on them.

Strange to say, he had some friends. In most towns the paper carriers and mail carriers are the first targets of a dog. But this one seemed to admire them as they went about their business delivering newspapers and mail. When others said angry things about him, the paper carriers only smiled. He was good company for them on their cold early morning or late afternoon routes.

He had other friends too. There were people who admired his spirit, his spunk, his cunning. Many a child without a pet looked at this dog and wondered if he could ever be tamed. Many a dog owner with a fat, satisfied pooch on the end of a leash paused beside a fire hydrant, looked up, saw that dog, and wondered if that was not what a real dog was supposed to be like.

But too many citizens were outraged at the thought that a dog like this could run loose in their town. The dog was in trouble.

3
Mayor Frederick

The Mayor of the town was a tall man who, in sunny or warm weather, walked to work, tapping the sidewalk with his walking stick. Occasionally he stabbed the air or just sliced it with his stick as he strode from his hillside home down through the town along Main Street to his office.

It was a pleasant October morning. The air was crisp and there was a spray of frost on the grass. The sun sat just above the horizon, making diamonds out of the frost. The forest which rimmed the town was in October colour, a medley of reds and yellows and greens. It was the kind of morning the Mayor liked and he smiled as he went along, saying good morning to everyone he met.

"Nice day, Mayor," they answered.

"Lovely," he replied.

He tapped the parking meters which his administration had installed. He paused to look into the window of a new store which his Engineering

Department had permitted. He was proud of the town he had helped build. It was his sixth term as mayor and he was proud of his office, proud of his citizens, proud even of the October morning, as though his Engineering Department had supplied that too.

The thing he liked best about his small town was that just about everyone knew everybody else, and of course they knew their mayor. He liked to listen to their complaints and act on them, or to soothe the complainers and advise them. So when he saw Mrs. Ottey standing at the municipal steps he knew he was going to have to give her a bit of his time, and he actually looked forward to it.

Mrs. Ottey was a widow, about sixty years old. She had been reduced to a family of only two cats and a dog. She often had complaints. At one time she had wanted the Mayor to do something about long-haired youths. Then she launched a campaign throughout the town trying to convince the citizens to adopt stray cats. She was that sort of woman.

The Mayor braced himself. "Good Morning, Mrs. Ottey."

" 'Mornin', Mayor."

He felt coldness in her voice. This wasn't going to be a trivial problem. Her hair was scrunched beneath a scarf; her eyes bored into him.

The Mayor looked around, scanning the town with

his eyes. "Isn't it a lovely morning for walking, Mrs. Ottey?"

She got right to the point. "When are you going to do something about that dog, Mayor Frederick?"

"Dog?" Mayor Frederick asked. "What dog?"

"The dog that's been running all over town and eating other dogs' food. And pickin' fights and maulin' other people's dogs."

"Is there such a dog?"

"And scaring people's cats and rushing at people and makin' other people's back yards his race course."

"Which dog is that?" asked the Mayor fiercely.

"It's nobody's, Mayor."

"Say that again. How can it be nobody's?"

She had to look up at him, this short, starchy lady with a faded scarf around her head.

"It's a *stray* dog, Mayor."

"And it's been doing all the things you say?"

"Yes, sir. It came out of nowhere. Nobody knows when he came but he's been worryin' everybody. He's been worryin' my cats and my dog and I can't keep any peace — "

"Outrageous!" said the Mayor. "And funny thing — funny thing that I am only hearing of him now. I will get our Dog Control Officer after him at once." Dog Control Officer was the Mayor's title for the dog-catcher.

When he took out his pocket diary and began to write in it, Mrs. Ottey already felt placated. The Mayor was going to do something about that dog. She knew it. He was a no-fooling-around kind of mayor. That was why she had been voting for him election after election.

"I'll act on it, Mrs. Ottey," he said. "Black-and-white, you say?" As he wrote he spoke under his breath. "Harries dogs and cats . . . fights . . . "

"Thank you, Mayor."

"Thank you, Mrs. Ottey, for bringing it to my attention. It's good citizens like you who keep a town the livable place it ought to be."

Mrs. Ottey was overwhelmed by such praise. Smiling widely, she said, "I'm depending on you, Mayor."

As the widow turned down the street on her way home, the Mayor mounted the steps to his office.

In fact, he was not at all ignorant of the dog. Who in the town had not heard of the black-and-white mutt that roamed about answering to no name? However, now that a citizen had confronted him with a complaint he would have to call up the Dog Control Officer and make this dog a priority. He could still hear Mrs. Ottey's shrill voice: "I'm depending on you, Mayor." And he could still see those hawk-like eyes of hers. And he knew perfectly well that every vote counted in a mayoral race.

4
The Dog Control Officer

By ten o'clock the dog-catcher was in the Mayor's office.

Rodney O'Malley was well fitted for his job, for he was a professional trapper. Dog-catching was merely a sideline. A man who was used to trapping beavers and otters, lynxes, martens and even the wily fox had no trouble catching mere dogs.

He was a small bald man whose size belied his vigour and strength. O'Malley, who also found time to guide moose hunters, could, it was reported, carry a quarter of a bull moose unassisted.

As he approached the Mayor's office he knocked out his pipe in his hand and threw the tobacco ash into the standing ash tray. He moved silently, surely. He was wearing mukluks and a plaid hunting jacket.

The Mayor's secretary directed the squat man into the inner office.

" 'Mornin', Mayor."

"Ah, O'Malley. I see you got my call."

"I came as soon as I heard, Mayor."

"Good man. Good man. Have a seat, O'Malley."

O'Malley took the nearest chair and sat on its edge. He knew the Mayor would not have called him in for something trivial.

"How's the trapping?" Mayor Frederick asked, deducing from the trapper's clothes that he had just returned from checking his traps.

O'Malley didn't like the question. It suggested that while he was out trapping he was neglecting his dog-catching duties. It was true that O'Malley pretended not to see many a dog. If a dog were too much in the public eye he would take it in, or if there were a complaint against one he would go after it. Otherwise he didn't hunt down loose dogs. The town council, which had made the by-law, agreed with this. After all, the town was like one big family. So O'Malley did not like Mayor Frederick's question about his trapping, and he did not answer.

The Mayor seemed pleasant enough as he peered over his glasses. "We've got a problem, O'Malley."

The trapper waited. By now he had guessed what the trouble was about, but he waited.

"It's nothing we can't lick, O'Malley. You're the best man I know to handle this — "

"A dog, Mayor?"

"Yes, a dog. A black-and-white fiend of a dog."

"Marauder?" O'Malley asked.

"What's that?"

"Marauder," O'Malley said again. "That's what some people been taggin' him with."

"Oh! So you've met with this marauder?"

"Not face to face, Mayor. But he is a dog with a reputation."

The Mayor, consulting his pocket diary, read from it. "Black-and-white . . . harries dogs and cats . . eats their suppers. . ."

"That's the one," O'Malley said. "Folks been calling me about him these couple o' days. 'What you going to do about that dog, O'Malley?' So I'll do something. But I still haven't seen the dog."

"You've never seen him?"

O'Malley shook his head.

"Hmm. 'Appears out of nowhere. . .has no owner. . . acts wild. . .' Is he big, I wonder?"

"Not according as I hear, Mayor."

"Mongrel most likely?"

"Most likely. Well, if I see him, I'll put him away right quick."

"Yes, yes. But we must do more than that, O'Malley."

"Huh?"

"We must make a point of seeing him. We can't let that dog become more of a celebrity than he already is."

"I'll do it," the trapper said, stiffening under the Mayor's words.

"That's my boy," the other said cheerfully.

O'Malley was a proud dog-catcher. He would act. But he knew that the job would not be easy, for this dog was somehow different from the others. It was clever, combining the instincts of something wild with the complete knowledge of human beings and their ways. He had a jumpy feeling in his chest that this dog would be a real test.

When he reached the steps he stopped and checked the streets, not for the dog, but to form a strategy and to ram tobacco into his pipe. As he lit up he remembered the Mayor's words: "We can't let that dog become more of a celebrity than he already is."

In quick, short strides he reached his pick-up truck. He pulled away from the curb fast, and in a short time pulled up in the driveway of his home on the edge of town.

It was one of the older houses, single-storied, with a brick chimney standing erect at one gable end. The paint was peeling from its white boards but there was a new addition in the back, with tarpaper still tacked to its plywood walls.

His wife, a bulky woman with a pleasant face, met him in the door. "Rodney, you're upset. What is it?"

"Nothing," he snapped.

"I'll make coffee," she said quietly but with

strength. O'Malley looked at her and said no more.

After a cup of coffee he got back into the truck and began to cruise slowly around town, looking for the dog. His net was in the back of the truck. He cruised for about half an hour, then drove up Main Street again. Turned into Deebe Lane. Down Cedar Row. Into Brick Lane. . .

Aha!

There he was, the marauding dog, trotting along the Canadian Pacific Railway main line. His easy gait and utter lack of concern maddened O'Malley.

"Now look at that," he said, stopping the truck. To the dog-catcher, a dog who had committed this many violations should have been looking over his shoulder. But not this one. He trotted along like a lord mayor of dogs, especially now that he was am- bling along a section of the line that rode on a trestle bridge, some several metres above the road on which O'Malley had stopped.

Getting out of the truck, O'Malley picked up the net. He would see what he could do.

Mr. Godfrey Aimes, whose back yard abutted on the railway line and who had been watching the carefree morning stroll of the dog with irritation, was happy to see O'Malley appear on the tracks.

"Wait, Rod," he called. "I'll give you a hand. You're aimin' to bag this rascal, ain't you?"

"Darn right," O'Malley said as he marched on his

muklukked legs towards the dog, which stood still, boldly assessing this new menace.

"Come on, you hound," coaxed O'Malley. "Come on. You're not going to run."

The dog stood his ground. He seemed to be studying O'Malley as if he wanted to remember this new one.

Then Mr. Aimes came over his fence behind the dog and climbed the slope to the tracks. He too had a net, not one for dog-catching but an old fishing net. He too was advancing stealthily, and from the rear. O'Malley moved in from the front.

At last the dog had enough of studying O'Malley. Turning suddenly, he beheld the other net carrier. Nearly caught, he had no time to study this new danger. He gave one defiant bark and ran down the grade. But the two men would not let him go so easily and gave chase.

"You wild fiend," Mr. Aimes cried. "You won't leave my Dandy alone. Wait until I lay a hand on you."

The dog had obviously been in the town long enough to know it well, for he headed for the open ball field where the chances of his being caught were slim. The two men, now angered by the obvious intelligence of the dog, refused to give up.

O'Malley, who was in vastly better shape than Aimes and younger besides, raced ahead and waved his arm to Aimes to make a detour and try to cut the dog off.

The dog seemed to be enjoying the chase. Suddenly he deserted the open field and headed downtown. The two would-be dog-catchers followed behind. With bold defiance the mutt trotted just ahead of them, alongside moving cars, in and out between parked ones, looking back occasionally to see how they were doing. He barked if they fell behind, and stopped, waiting for them.

People were beginning to stop on the sidewalk and stare. At last Mr. Aimes dropped out of the chase. He was out of breath. O'Malley was still in hot pursuit. After all, he was the dog-catcher. He was in the public eye. He could not, must not, give up.

So down the length of Main Street they went.

"Give a hand here!" he called out, puffing now. "Cut him off!"

Up the street they went again. Then the dog led poor O'Malley down the alley beside a hotel. Here there was a wide circular mud puddle. The water was clear, and it was time for a drink. With the assurance of a winner, the dog stopped on the near side and began to lap water. O'Malley, exhausted, caught up. Desperately he threw his net. The dog side-stepped. It missed. Then O'Malley slipped in the mud, and before he could steady himself, he splashed face downwards in the puddle.

The few spectators who had caught up laughed as the short man raised himself up, wiping the soupy mud from his face and moustache. The dog stood well back and barked, walked on, then turned and barked again. It was as though he too were laughing.

He had won, but from now on he had the most dangerous enemy a dog could possibly have.

5
Houdini

Deep in disgust, shame and mud, O'Malley gave up and made for home. He was in a barking mood himself and snapped at his wife.

"Coffee!" he demanded.

She wiped her hands on her apron. "What's the matter, Rodney? What's wrong?"

"Coffee," he repeated.

She plugged in the kettle. She knew that something awful had happened to her man by his clothes and face. Had he been in a fight? Or had he only fallen in the mud? She didn't ask again.

Soon O'Malley was drinking his third cup of coffee. He stood by the window looking out at nothing. Finally he was ready to talk, although he wasn't really confiding in his wife. He was merely speaking out loud, letting his frustrations out, and she happened to hear.

"Danged dog!" he said. "Shamed me. Made fun of me. I'll get him," he vowed.

"What dog, Rod?"

"Just a dog."

"He must be a mighty tough one." She spoke softly, unlike O'Malley, who was loud and brittle in his speech. She was plump, he was lean; she stood well above his short frame.

"Black-and-white?" she asked.

He snorted and sat down at the table again.

"A new dog in town? Always fighting other dogs?" she asked.

"Danged dog," he repeated morosely.

"Yes, there's a lot o' talk about him," she said.

"I'll get him," he said, flipping the pages of a reader their only son Red had left on the table. Red was in school. "They complain, then they won't lend a hand," he continued. "Never mind. I'll get him." He looked down at himself. "Led me into a mud puddle," he said.

Lifting the lid from one of the steaming pots on the stove, she stirred the contents around, then dipped up a spoonful and tasted it.

O'Malley got up.

"Don't wander far. Lunch'll be ready soon."

"I ain't hungry."

She did not argue; she rarely did. This was one of his bad days. Out in the driveway he picked up his net from his truck.

Mr. Aimes, who was keeping an eye on O'Malley's

door, stepped out and met him on the sidewalk.

O'Malley felt Aimes had ruined his first effort. He hated to meet the man a second time, yet here he was.

"Havin' another go at him, Rod?"

"Darn right I am."

"I'll get my net."

"Don't have to, Godfrey."

"What are friends for, Rod? Besides I have more than a passin' interest in that dog. He's been worryin' my Dandy a lot."

"Suit yourself," O'Malley grunted.

O'Malley was wise in the ways of dogs. He had decided that this dog would be having a noon-hour nap now. And such a wanted dog with no yard of his own to sleep in would find himself a no-dog's land for his nap. So O'Malley began to work his way along the rail line, looking for such a place. Suddenly he froze, motioning Aimes to be quiet.

He pointed to the culvert beneath them. The culvert conducted ditch water under the railway, but now the ditch was dry. It was an ideal place for a dog to take a nap.

A strategy was hastily mapped out. Mr. Aimes took up his position at one end while O'Malley slipped down to block the other. Sure enough, when they both stooped and looked into the large pipe at the same time, they saw their quarry.

But he was not sleeping now, for the hunters had awakened him. His head was up, his ears erect.

"Your net!" O'Malley shouted at Aimes. "Block your end up!"

They both blocked the exits at the same time.

By now the dog had realized his desperate situation. He would have to do something, and the sooner, the better. He stood stiff-legged, every muscle tensed. Wheeling in the tunnel, he seemed to be sizing up each face that peered at him from behind a net. While he pondered, he snarled. Did he detect indecision in Mr. Aimes? Barking and showing a set of nasty white fangs, he rushed at him.

Mr. Aimes was not a dog-catcher. He wanted the dog caught, but not enough to get himself bitten.

Besides, the barrel of the culvert amplified the dog's barks. The white teeth flashed in the gloom. Aimes pulled back instinctively and the dog shot free.

Furious, O'Malley began to shout at Aimes as he raced up the slope chasing the dog along the railway tracks. This time, however, he was gaining on his quarry. The dog's recent sleep had left him groggy and slow.

From behind them a train approached, slowing down to stop at the station. Its bell was clanging, but O'Malley paid it no mind except to make sure he was out of the way. He continued to gain on the dog.

The train was running alongside them now, the man, the dog and the train all moving in the same direction. The train slowed more and more, but it was still in motion when the dog stopped, leapt aboard a flatcar, almost lost his footing, then scrambled back upright.

Turning, he barked once at O'Malley before he jumped off the far side, safe and sound and free.

Blocked from his quarry by the moving train, O'Malley threw down his net in an awesome rage and stormed at the train, the dog and Godfrey Aimes.

But although Aimes had been left far behind, he had nonetheless seen the unusual escape and was impressed. He rushed up to where O'Malley stood.

"Did you see that, Rodney?" he shouted. "What an escape! That dog is a — superdog!"

The word "superdog" and the respect with which Aimes uttered it made O'Malley suddenly loathe Godfrey Aimes. A great help he was, praising the dog he had helped to escape. Speechless, O'Malley turned his back on Aimes and strode back to the house.

But Aimes began to admire the dog that was so human in its behaviour, so clever in its escapes, an underdog that had outsmarted two such clever dog-catchers.

Instead of going home, Aimes went right to the Prattley Hotel. He felt like talking. He knew a legend was being born, and he knew that he was part of it.

This soon after opening time the hotel had only a few customers, but Aimes spotted two of his friends sitting at a table and joined them. Big Finn, a retired lumberjack and one of the men who went to the hotel regularly, brought out his wallet. "Sit down, Godfrey. I'll buy you a drink."

After Aimes had emptied his glass, he began to praise the superdog.

"Greatest dog there is. Nobody — nobody will catch that one! Not O'Malley for sure. No, sir. You should've seen what he did to us. We got him cornered, see? In the culvert. Two nets, one at each end. And we thought we had him. But I tell you, he came barrelling out of the culvert and I had to give. He's got teeth on him like a wolf. I was glad to give way.

"Then we chased him up the tracks. The train was comin' in. You boys heard it come in? A freight train, a long one. We chased him along the train, and you should've seen that dog. He hopped on the moving train — "

"Come on, Godfrey. Hopped aboard a train? A dog?"

"That's it boys. It's the truth! You never heard of a dog that hopped on a train before? Well, this one did! Hopped right on to a flatcar, looked round at O'Malley and grinned at him. Yessir, that was a grin! Then he barked at him, and then the darn dog jumped off on the other side safe and free. I tell you, that dog is an escape-artist, that's a fact! Yessir — a real escape-artist, just like Houdini!"

And that was how the superdog got his name — Houdini.

6
Superdog

For O'Malley, the next weeks were wretched ones. The dog became an obsession with him. As he spent more and more time roaming the town trying to find and catch Houdini, his trapping business suffered, for his traps were not checked regularly. Yet he had no luck catching the dog. Houdini remained free.

O'Malley found that he couldn't even relax at the local hotel without having some joker make wisecracks about the dog.

"Seen that superdog around today, O'Malley?"

"Houdini catch any trains today, Dog-Catcher?"

He found out too that the hotel patrons were betting on the day Houdini would be caught, and even about whether he would be caught at all.

O'Malley began to avoid public places. He wouldn't answer the phone. He was surly to his family. His wife kept quiet and his son stayed away from home as much as possible.

Meanwhile Houdini was gaining admirers. God-frey Aimes, for example. Although he continued to love and care for his own dog Dandy, he said he had to give credit where credit was due. That was some dog.

Among the children Houdini won many friends. The idea of a superdog caught their imagination and they spent endless hours at school drawing him on the covers of their scribblers and on the tops of their desks. Houdini was shown whipping a whole pack of huge dogs, hopping aboard a fast moving diesel, mocking the dog-catcher.

After school, fans of the superdog pinned posters of him on O'Malley's fence, a prank which made the little man even angrier, even more humiliated. Some also chalked taunts on the sidewalks outside his house:

From underdog to superdog
*

Houdini — dog escape-artist
*

Quit hounding Houdini

One local poet wrote a song about the dog:

Houdini!
A dog named Houdini
Black-and-white devil
Smart as a fox
Quick as a goat.

Houdini!
A dog named Houdini
Led catcher O'Malley
To a sprawl in a puddle.

Houdini!
A dog named Houdini
Cornered in a culvert
But came out like a
bullet.

Houdini!
A dog named Houdini
Hopped on a train
To the dog-catcher's
shame.

One boy, Tommy Wren, went home one day and asked his mother if his dog could have pups for superdog.

"Pups?" asked the startled mother.

"Yes. I want him for their daddy," the child explained.

"No, Tommy!" cried his mother. "We don't want any pups of that rascal in this house! Go wash up for dinner."

But parents could not squelch their children's respect for the dog. Cans of dogfood disappeared from cupboards at a remarkable rate as children secretly fed him. He began to live very well indeed.

Houdini made friends among the adults too. He was the most talked-about dog the town had ever had and some began to hope that he would continue to evade O'Malley. He was the subject of endless conversations. People wondered where he had come from, how he had got so smart, how long he would evade the dog-catcher. He gave the people something to laugh about and something to bet on. Of course, now that he was being fed by so many of the town's children, he had little need for stealing other dogs' food or fighting with them. Naturally resentment towards him cooled.

But not everyone was his friend. The grade four teacher, Mr. Ogden, for example. His dog, a purebred collie without a whit of courage, had been publicly whipped by the stray dog when he first arrived in town. Mr. Ogden, therefore, was not at all amused when children began defacing their desks — a forbidden activity at any time — with pictures of that rascally tramp dog.

Then he caught Willie Benson carving Houdini's name into the window sill by the pencil sharpener. Mr. Ogden was furious and told Willie he would have to pay to have the damage repaired. Willie went home crying and asked his father for the money. Unfortunately Mr. Benson had been out of work for two months and was in no mood to hand over any money. He marched off to the school and angrily accosted Mr. Ogden as he sat in his classroom after school marking notebooks.

The teacher looked up as the door was flung open.

"Ah, Mr. Benson," he said, rising.

But Mr. Benson was not in a talking mood.

"You'll get not one cent of money from me," he shouted angrily. "You bleed me dry in my taxes already!"

"But Mr. Benson — "

"And that dog of yours is a yellow coward, and the superdog is worth ten of him. And if you're such a wonderful teacher, why don't you teach your dog to fight?"

At that Mr. Ogden forgot he was a teacher and got mad. When the principal, attracted by the noise, came bursting into the room, he found Mr. Ogden and Mr. Benson standing only whiskers apart, shouting in each other's face and emphasizing each insult with a shove or a push.

The principal got Mr. Ogden out of there fast and calmed Mr. Benson down with the promise that Willie could repair the damage himself with sandpaper, thus saving his father the money. At the next staff meeting he reminded the staff that they were professionals and that they must always be calm.

The other teachers were furious. They said that if a teacher could be attacked in his classroom for merely doing his duty something was wrong somewhere. They urged that all writers of graffiti about that dog should be suspended immediately.

The principal replied that indeed they had a problem with graffiti and doodles, but over-reacting was only adding fuel to the fire. He looked at Mr. Ogden when he said this. Mr. Ogden looked out the window. Back in the classrom Willie was sanding away quietly.

But that was not all. Many of the other students in Mr. Ogden's room were furious at Willie for getting their favourite teacher into trouble. They felt Willie should not have run to his father. In fact, they called him a rat-fink, which led to a fight in the playground at recess. Soon the father of the boy who fought Willie was also involved in a feud with Mr. Benson.

Then the story got to the school board, for Mr. Benson wanted Mr. Ogden fired. The school board said they would look into the situation. Mr. Ogden was not fired, though he was cautioned about controlling his temper.

Everyone had an opinion on the subject. Some were for Mr. Ogden and wrote letters to the local newspaper giving their support. Others criticized him in letters to the board. The town was divided.

The Mayor sat in his office as the controversy raged through his town. He had only one question. *Why was that dog still loose?*

7
A Plan

To add to the injury, Houdini boldly began to hang out in the vacant lot beside O'Malley's back yard. The dog-catcher was infuriated by this to the point where his wife feared for what the dog might do to her husband's nerves and his trapping business. But Houdini knew precisely what he was doing. He had come to rank O'Malley as Enemy Number One. From his vantage point he could watch the dog-catcher's movements, which put O'Malley at a disadvantage.

Was the superdog making fun of him? People made jokes about a dog-catcher with a stray mutt camping out beside his back yard.

The Mayor was furious. He called O'Malley in.

"What do you think we look like?" he stormed. "Laughing stocks, that's what. Do something, man!"

"You want me to shoot him?" O'Malley asked.

"Good grief, no. That would be political suicide."

"I'm no politician, Mayor. I'm just a dog-catcher — Dog Control Officer to you. And shooting controls any dog."

"We'd have everybody on our backs. Shooting a dog! Good heavens, no. Don't you know the by-laws of this town? Don't you know that the use of firearms inside the town limits is unlawful?"

O'Malley was unmoved. "I could poison him."

"O'Malley!" The Mayor threw up his arms. He paced the floor as he spoke. "You're positively mad. Poison? No, no, no! But — wait a minute. Wait a dog-gone minute."

Gradually the Mayor's anger turned to hope. "Poison, you say? No, not poison. Something else, O'Malley. We'll do him in yet! We'll use something else, something better. Something less offensive. Not to kill him, just to. . .I saw it on televison. Why didn't we think of this before? Tranquillizers, O'Malley. Tranquillizers! That will fix him, won't it? Sure it will."

O'Malley's eyes were shining and a faint smile pulled his face up.

"Fix him some in a meal," the Mayor went on. "That dog will stuff it in and topple over asleep. You see it on TV every day, only they use a gun to deliver the tranquillizer. We'll fix him, won't we, O'Malley?"

"It's a good idea, Mayor," O'Malley agreed.

Pleased with himself, the Mayor strode around his

office. "Now I'll get those people off my back. Off your back as well."

O'Malley was smiling broadly now. He shook the Mayor's hand. "Will do, Mayor," he said. "Will do." Before he left he accepted one of the Mayor's cigars.

Out on the steps again he watched snowflakes drift down from the clouds. He had always liked snow but he liked it twice as much now. He felt happy, and when he was happy he liked everything twice as much.

He began to murmur to himself. "Superdog, eh? Houdini, they call you. I'll feed you so much sleepiness you won't take four steps before you keel over. Your days are numbered, mongrel dog."

Because O'Malley did not keep tranquillizers in stock, he could not bait Houdini's food on that day. The municipality would have to order some. But the next day. The next day, the next day, superdog.

Lightheartedly he went to check his traps and as he pluffed through the snow on snowshoes his thoughts matched his vigorous sweeping strides.

From superdog to sleeping dog —
I'll get you at last;
Left me sprawling in mud.
Came flying out of a culvert.
Jumped on a flatcar.

Setting up house next to my back yard. . .
Letting them sing songs about you,
And draw pictures of you;
but I'll get you, Houdini. . .
Get you with tranquil dog food.
Then you'll be a sleeping dog.
And I'll let the sleeping dog be. . .

He felt better than he had in weeks. He was a new man. The idea of tranquillizers had made him creative, even poetic. So many times had he ploughed through the snow, so many times had he been in the woods and they had been just snow and trees to him. But now he saw them with a fresh eye.

The crunching snow was a glittering carpet beneath the bright sun. The trees were pretty with it, cupping patches of it in their branches. And the trees themselves — how cathedral-like.

His traps had caught a rich harvest — three beavers, a red fox, seven martens and an otter.

"My luck has turned," he said aloud. "Now I'll get him."

Back at home he was bubbly and warm. He even called his wife "Love," much to her surprise. She hadn't seen him this way for a long time.

He was skinning the animals, working in the annex which adjoined the kitchen. It was a large room, added for just this purpose of skinning animals and hanging the pelts. It was heated by a wood stove which sputtered loudly. As he skinned the first beaver he hummed merrily to himself.

"You caught the dog, Rod." She made it a statement instead of a question.

"Not yet, dear. Not yet. But I will. I got a plan."

"I sure hope you catch him."

He looked up. "You mean that?"

"Of course I mean it," she said.

"You must be one of the few."

"Oh?" she asked.

"Whole town is infatuated with that mongrel dog. Even my friends secretly love him. Godfrey Aimes even — whole lot o' them. Superdog they call him. Houdini. Of all things — *Houdini!*" He was scornful.

"I've heard. I don't like a dog making fun of my husband," she said. "And the people! Happy that a dog makes fun of a man. I'll pour you another coffee."

Picking up his empty cup, she stepped back into the kitchen. "I'm with you, Rod. It's not right for a dog to be acting like that. It's not right for it to be eating into you like this."

Her words made him feel even better. He sipped his coffee as he went on skinning.

About this time Red O'Malley came home from school. "Hi, Mom," he said, dropping his school bag in the nearest corner. "Pop home yet?"

"Yes."

The boy poked his head around the door of the annex. The sight of the animals lying on the side table and the skinning taking place under the skilled hands of his father made his eyes brighten. "Hi, Pop," he said.

"Hi," said his father.

Growing bolder, Red stepped into the room and cautiously began to explore the deep furs of the animals lying there. When he pulled away his hands they were wet from the thawed snow. Then he began to weigh each animal in his hand.

"Can I go with you next time, Pop?"

"Nope."

"This weekend?"

"Nope."

"Gee, you never take me with you. Not even on weekends."

"Go do your school work."

"Can't I just stay and watch?"

"Out!"

"Aw." The disappointed boy scuffed out.

His mother met him at the door. "Don't bother your father, Red."

"I wasn't bothering him."

"Go and do your homework."

"It's done already," he told his mother. "I did it at school."

"Well, bring in some firewood for your father's stove."

"Yes, Mom."

After changing into work clothes, Red dutifully began to fetch firewood from the stack outside. He unloaded it into the wood box slowly, giving himself a chance to watch his father skinning and stretching.

As soon as he was finished he vanished from the house. He would go and see his friend, Alty, unless Alty and his father had gone off on their snowmobile. He wished his family had a snowmobile. But what would be the use? His dad would probably not take him out anyway, nor let him ride it alone.

Working skilfully, O'Malley once again felt the joy of victory flood through him. The Mayor was looking after the tranquillizer. It would be in his hands tomorrow. Tonight he could sleep light. He knew that tonight the dog would have one last night of good sleep. Then he would sleep forever. For tomorrow he would have him, and since he had no owner, he would then be destroyed.

Goodbye, superdog. Goodbye, Houdini!

8

Red O'Malley

Red O'Malley was a loner. His one friend, Alty McGregor, lived four blocks away. That's where he headed now.

He heard and saw boys playing street hockey on Purvis Street but he did not try to join them. In fact, he went down a back street to avoid them, though they probably wouldn't have asked him to play even if he had gone and stood right at the edge of the game.

Red did not like team sports. Skating he could tolerate, but hockey he hated. What made it bad was that Red knew his father wanted him to play hockey the way all the other boys in town did. O'Malley somehow felt Red had let him down because he didn't. All the other men boasted about their sons. But he had nothing to brag about in return.

Red was not in love with baseball either, although he played it at school each spring when his teacher took the class out to the ball diamond. All through the year he played team sports, but only at school, only when he had to.

There were two sports he truly loved though — fishing and hunting. Fishing he could do from the town dock and he knew all the good spots in the creek and river which flowed through the town. But he was not old enough to go hunting by himself. He would have loved to go along with his father when he went to hunt deer and moose each year, but his father never took him. Red had never even seen his father fire a gun.

If only he had a dog it wouldn't be so bad. Then he would have company on his long hikes through the woods. If he had a dog he could train it to track and fetch. . . Red sighed. Lots of boys had a dog, but not the dog-catcher's son.

He knocked on Alty's door. Alty's sister answered. She was a nice girl with curly dark hair and lots of colour in her cheeks. Polite, smiling.

Alty was not at home, she said. He had gone to the next town with his father. They would be back around nightfall.

"Do you want to wait? *The Flintstones* are on."

"No thanks, Margaret. I'll come back later."

"Are you sure?"

"Yes. Or I'll phone Alty tonight."

Red moved away fast. That was crazy. He couldn't go downstairs and watch TV with Alty's sister! His cheeks were flushed and he felt warm. She sure had a nice smile though.

He hesitated. Alty was not home but he could — instead he would — He heard the snowmobiles buzzing along the golf course on the edge of town. He would take a look.

The sun was gone but there would be time enough. He certainly did not want to go back to his house just yet. He wished he had a brother, or a sister like Margaret. Or if he had a dog they could be out here walking along doing nothing together.

As he neared the golf course the *rat-tat* of the machines grew louder and he could see them skimming atop the snow, riding the bumps as a boat does a wave. He saw the snow powder churn beneath their tracks and he saw the scarves of the riders fly in the wind behind them. Standing aside, he watched, fascinated.

He took shelter from the wind in the lee of an old cabin which had once belonged to a trapper. That was before the town had grown outwards and before the golf course had been hacked out of the forest. But the cabin still stood, durable and almost eternal, its chimney jutting up above its rotting shingled roof. One of its windows was broken, shattered by the bullet of an unsuccessful hunter. There was a door, but it was not locked and Red went inside. No one had done any damage here. A wooden table lay on its side and an old hat hung from a nail beside the door. There was a wooden poster bed, a stone fireplace, shelves and a woodbox.

Red went to the broken window and looked out, watching the snowmobiles. They were fast, they had power. They could manoeuvre. He wished he could have a fast ride on one, but he didn't know any of the drivers well enough to ask them for one.

Not all of the machines were skimming along at top speed. One was moving slower. It was a father giving his children a ride. One child rode on the machine behind his father while two more sat in a sleigh that he was pulling. It reminded Red of the ducks that swam just ahead of the ducklings in early spring.

The light was fading fast.

Suddenly Billy Wren emerged from the woods. He was pulling a Christmas tree on a sled. It was a lovely tree and it gave Red an idea. Why not take home a tree himself? Taking home a tree would be a good idea. It would please his mother and give him an excuse for going home a bit late. Quickly he left the cabin, closing the door carefully behind him.

Countless times in the spring and summer he had taken home fish, rainbow or speckled trout or delicious pickerel. Something for the larder never failed to please his mother. Usually she forgot even to ask him where he had been. In the winter months he often brought home rabbits which he snared. But now it was time for a Christmas tree.

He spotted the axe that Billy had used to cut his tree.

"Nice tree, Billy," he said.

"Not bad," Billy responded. He was wearing a parka jacket and his ears were covered by the flaps of his cap. His trouser legs were tucked snugly into heavy snow-covered snowmobile boots. "What you doing out here?"

"Oh, nothing. Came to get a tree too, but forgot to

bring an axe."

Billy agreed to lend him his. "I know where there's another good one," he said. "Come on, I'll show you."

"Thanks," Red said.

Leaving his tree behind, Billy led the way into the snow-deep forest where every tree, large and small, held large lumps of snow in its branches. Here there was only silence. Even the noise of the snowmobiles barely penetrated.

Soon they returned with Red's tree on the sled. They strapped Billy's on top of it and together pulled the heavy sled home.

Dusk was now darkening the hills but the snow reflected so much light that out in the open Red could see easily. The riders still raced about on their snowmobiles. The boys' boots crunched on the packed snow on the trail. Then the lights of the town began to greet them, twinkling in the gathering darkness. The added decorations of coloured lights which hung along eaves and gable ends glittered cheerfully.

They reached Billy's house first and he unloaded his tree and lent Red his sled to take the second tree home. Red would return it tomorrow. He made for home but when he got to Alty's house he noticed Mr. McGregor's pick-up truck in the driveway. Alty was back.

It was now full dark, but who said that he couldn't

pop in for a while and see Alty? He would see
Margaret too, and get another of her smiles. He was
feeling cold, and Margaret and Alty's house always
seemed warmer than home.

It was Margaret who got the door again. "He's in
the basement," she said. "Come on in. Look at all
that snow on you!"

This was her polite way of telling Red he needed to
brush the loose snow off his clothing. He used the
broom that was left in the porch for just such a
reason, and took off his snowy boots.

Alty was in the basement and there on the floor,
lying on its back and kicking four legs at Alty's
fingers and growling puppy growls, was one of the
finest pups Red had ever seen.

"Hi, Red," Alty said, looking up.

"What's that?" Red asked.

Alty grinned. "It's a puppy. Got him this afternoon. Pop bought him. Isn't he cute?"

Red just stared. "He's yours?" he asked at last. "All yours?"

"Uh-huh. A pre-Christmas present!"

Red was silent. What wouldn't he give for a pup like that? He felt jealousy flooding through him, a fierce longing for a pup of his own. He couldn't stay here any longer.

"Got to run," he said.

"Don't you want to pet him?" Alty asked.

"Not tonight, Alty. I'm late. Tomorrow, maybe."

"I'm calling him Samson," said Alty, grabbing a small front paw.

"Yeah? Nice name. Got to run now. See you, Alty, See you, Margaret." He had completely forgotten about her until now.

"See you," they both said.

Red pulled the sled home swiftly, his breath smoking in front of him. It was quite dark when he got there.

"Where've you been, Red?" his mother asked. "Good grief, boy — "

"Went to get a tree, Mom. That's all."

He lifted the tree into the house, dragging it down to the basement where the snow on the needles and branches would melt before they put it up. She followed him down and watched him lean it up in a corner. She was pleased, just as he had hoped.

"It's a good tree," she said. "You must have been far."

"Yes," he said.

"You hungry?" she asked.

"Not much," he replied.

That pup Samson had taken away his hunger for food.

"Where's Pop?" he asked.

Turning her eyes up, she said, "Watching TV."

He could hear the set and the excitement in the announcer's voice. It was *Hockey Night in Canada*, Philadelphia Flyers versus Toronto in Maple Leaf Gardens. Pop would be glued to the set. He was a Toronto fan. Red could have stayed out a couple of hours later and he wouldn't have been scolded, not when his pop watched hockey.

Red had to ask. "Why can't I have a dog, Mom?"

"You heard what your father said."

"But he doesn't say anything. All he says is no."

"He's a dog-catcher, Red. How would it look if a dog from his house begins to run loose?"

"But it won't. I wouldn't let it."

"Come on, supper's on the table."

They climbed out of the basement and Red ate supper while he thought of the exact words he would say to his father.

After supper he was all ready. He waited for a commercial. "Pop," he said, "guess what I want for Christmas?"

"What?" his father asked, puffing on his pipe. He was in a mellow mood. Toronto had just scored.

"A pup!"

"No way."

"Lots of boys have dogs."

"Nope."

"Alty has a pup. He just got it — for Christmas. His dad bought it for him."

"No dogs in this house," his father said.

"Ah, Pop. I wouldn't let it run loose. It wouldn't embarrass you."

"Enough, boy."

The game had resumed. Red knew it was useless. In frustration he stormed to his room.

He too was a fan of Houdini's. He too had drawn the dog many times. But he had kept the pictures hidden in a box in his closet. He did not work at them in the house or even look at them there, out of respect for his father. But he was angry enough now to be reckless. He took them from the box and unfolded them, then taped them to the walls beside the other pictures already there: pictures of racing cars that he had drawn and coloured, pictures of fish he had cut from magazines, pictures of two huskies and an arctic wolf.

Satisfied, he lay flat on his stomach on the bed, kicking his feet, first the left and then the right. Let him come, he thought defiantly. Let Pop come and see that his own son was a fan of Houdini.

But it was his mother who came upstairs to check on him, for she felt his deep frustration, his sadness, his loneliness.

"What're you doing?"

"Oh — nothing. Just lying here."

"Someday you'll have a dog."

"When? When I grow up and it doesn't matter anymore?" he asked harshly.

"Don't talk to me like that, son."

"Sorry, Mom." It was not *her* fault.

When she turned to go she saw the pictures. The wonder dog stood on hind legs and beat a lion-like chest with boxing-gloved front paws; bold letters in alternating colours of red and green said — *Houdini*.

"Red, what's this? Do you want your father to skin you alive?"

He might as well, Red thought.

But his mother thought otherwise, and with frantic fingers she peeled the drawings off the wall.

"Hide them, boy! Destroy them! What in the world made you do that?"

"He's my hero, Mom."

"A dog? A dog is your hero?"

"He's everybody's."

"But he makes fun of your dad. He torments your own father."

"Mom," Red said, sitting up, eager to make her understand, "he's a wonder dog. No kidding. The best. I wish I had a dog like that."

As though she expected her husband to come barging in at any moment, his mother kept an eye on the door.

"You destroy these tomorrow," she said, holding out the pictures, "and never bring them into this house again!"

But Red would not promise.

"Then I'll destroy them."

Mrs. O'Malley slipped them inside her blouse.

"You should have more consideration for your father," she said sternly. "Of all the dogs in this town, you have to draw pictures of that one. But his days are numbered!"

That made Red glance sharply at her. "How?" was all he asked.

"Your dad has what will fix him. It's just a matter of time now."

"What has he got?"

"Tranquillizers, that's what. They'll knock him out, then he'll be captured and this whole disgrace will end."

"Oh no," Red whispered.

"Whose side are you on, Red?"

"It's not fair," Red said. "Can't you see, Mom? Houdini hasn't ever done any harm."

She left the room then. She hated to upset him, but the sooner he got that dog out of his heart the better.

Red went to bed, but slept little that night.

9
Caught

It was Christmas week and the town was getting ready for the festivities. Fathers and sons plunged into the woods that ringed the town and returned pulling Christmas trees on sleds. House eaves were trimmed with coloured lights and so were the evergreens that stood on front lawns.

The lawns had another kind of decoration, snowmen with carrot noses and scarves around their necks. Some children built forts.

The snowdrifts were sand-dune high and lay white and pure as cirrus clouds. The only dirty spots were where the graders had pushed the snow back from the roadway. There, gravel and dirt lay embedded in the banks. Where salt had been scattered, it had eaten holes in the ice until the roads resembled honeycombs. But the fields were untouched. Beneath the trees were two-metre depths of snow, marked only by the pattering feet of rabbits and the silent paws of predators.

The stores were decorated with tinsel, paper bells and balloons. Business was brisk. Toddlers' eyes sparkled as they guessed what was hidden in the packages their parents brought home.

In a special place in refrigerators, huge Christmas turkeys lay waiting. Mothers were baking.

Loggers who stayed a week at a time in the bush camps began to arrive in town early. They would not work again for several days.

Spirits in the town began to lift. After all, Christmas is special, a time when people willingly forget grudges, forgive wrongs and smile at strangers. In the festive spirit that prevailed in the town, Houdini was all but forgotten by everyone except one person — Dog Control Officer O'Malley.

He had obtained the tranquillizer and had given it one try already, but had failed in his attempt to capture the dog. He had thought that Houdini, a hungry stray, would gobble up any food offered to him, but he was wrong. He had put the drug in some leftover soup, but the dog had merely stopped, sniffed it and walked on. He had just had a mess of bones behind one of the food stores and a couple of handouts from secret food dishes and was much too full to try O'Malley's unappetizing dish.

The dog-catcher, who had been watching from his kitchen window, was furious when he saw the dog reject the drugged food.

"That devil!" he growled. "Too good to eat soup, is he? I'll teach him!" and he stamped his foot so hard that the crockery in the cupboards rattled. Suddenly he was struck with a new fear. What if the dog could smell the tranquillizer and refused to eat the bait?

That night he could not sleep, and he arose from bed short-tempered and irritable. He suspected he was going to have a rotten Christmas. But he wouldn't give up, not just yet.

From the woods he brought in two freshly snared rabbits. He hung them in the basement so they would thaw, then he cleaned them and cut them up. No more scraps for Houdini. Tonight he would dine on rabbit stew prepared especially for him.

O'Malley made the rabbit stew himself on the stove in the room where he skinned and stretched pelts. When it had cooled he doped it and set it out in the back yard, back against the fence so that Houdini would find it without any trouble. Then he kept watch. If another dog stumbled on the rich food he would be there to chase him away. If Houdini gulped it down, he would be there to get him. So he waited.

Houdini did come by, stepping briskly, his tail held high, the king of dogs. From the Canadian Pacific rails he smelled the rabbit stew when he paused to test the air. One sniff told him where the delicious smell came from. When he spied the dish, he broke

into a trot and headed straight for it.

As though he sensed something was wrong, he walked around the bait twice, but he couldn't resist it. He had not yet made his dinner rounds. He was hungry and this smelled too good to walk away from.

Somewhere he had smelled this aroma before, somewhere he had tasted rabbit. Yes, that old man, the one who had owned him. Old Man Raith — he used to cook the stuff. Delicious stuff. And after that, after the old man had gone away, he, Houdini, had caught himself some of that meat. Yes, he remembered.

He dug in.

"Hallelujah!" cried O'Malley and squeezed his fists together. He was smiling broadly. His wife, who had been watching with him, was happy for him.

"Rodney," she said. "At last."

He kissed her quickly, a rare deed for him. He even danced around the kitchen. Then abruptly he said, "I've got work to do. I've got to get him." Quickly he pulled on his mukluks.

Houdini ate ravenously and licked the bowl clean. Then he turned towards the tracks. But when he tried to go up the slope he found that he could not. His legs would not obey him; they did not even want to hold him up. And his eyes! They were dimming. The surroundings got suddenly darker.

Faintly he heard O'Malley slam the porch door behind him. He turned and in a blur saw his enemy, the man, coming nearer. So *he* was the one.

Houdini barked once, faintly. He tried to get away. Since he could not go up the slope, he took the easier way. He ran blindly in another direction, between some buildings, then onto a street.

O'Malley gave chase. Thanks to the dog's drugged condition, the dog-catcher was gaining rapidly. It seemed that he was going to lay hands on Houdini any moment when suddenly the dog turned a corner and vanished! O'Malley began to search for him behind the garbage cans and garages in the back lane, into which he had seen Houdini turn. But the dog was no longer in the vicinity. He had slipped down a side passage and was already on the next street, running blindly, stumbling.

That was when the car hit him.

Red O'Malley was standing right there when it happened. He was on top of a high grader-made snowbank on Marks Road, poised on the skis his parents had given him for Christmas the year before. He was waiting for the oncoming car to go by so he could ski down and across the road. From where he stood he saw Houdini come stumbling across the street, right into the path of the car.

"Houdini!" Red yelled. "Look out!"

But the dog could no longer hear or see anything. He was already asleep on his legs. There was a thumping sound as the bumper sent him sprawling into the snow at Red's feet. The car skidded out of control and spun into the snowbank about ten metres up the street.

Houdini did not utter a sound. Red thought he was dead, but he knelt quickly and felt the dog for a sign of life. Houdini was breathing.

Two men got out of the car.

"Did I kill him?" one asked.

"You couldn't help it," the other said. "Dog ran right out into the road."

They saw Red bending over the dog.

"Is he dead, kid?"

"No," Red said.

"The dog yours?"

"Yes," Red lied.

"Think I'll give the kid a couple o' bucks, Ossie. What the heck? It's Christmas."

"Dogs got no right on the streets," Ossie said. "There's a by-law about dogs running loose."

Red's mind was working fast now. He remembered his father and the tranquillizers. That ex-

plained Houdini's slow and stumbling gait. If the dog were doped, wouldn't it mean that his father was just behind? If he were to save Houdini he had better get the dog out of there.

He was lucky no one was on the street except the two men who had been riding in the car. They were now busy trying to get the vehicle dislodged from the snowbank. One was revving the engine while the other pushed. The black wheels spun ineffectively on the ice.

Red tried to lift the drugged and wounded dog but he could not. The dead weight was too much for him. But he could drag him easily on the snow. This he did, and not a moment too soon, for just as he had pulled the dog over the summit of the snowbank and onto the other side out of sight his father arrived, hot on Houdini's trail.

"Where could he be?" O'Malley asked himself. "Vanish just like that? Impossible."

Red thought furiously. He could not escape with Houdini, but he could hide him. He took off his jacket and covered the dog, and then he dug the snow with his mittened hands. Soon he had heaped enough of it to cover the dog completely. The snow was light and flaky. Houdini would not suffocate.

It was best to clear out of the area, so Red took off on his skis and went home fast.

It was dark when he got there. From the street his house looked Christmasy and pretty with lights blinking on and off along the eaves. Through the picture window he could see the tree he and his mother had decorated, the tinsel glistening in the light.

When he opened the door his mother turned quickly. "Rodney?" she called.

"It's me, Mom," Red said

She had hoped it would be her husband with the drugged dog. But it was only Red.

"Did you see your father?"

"No," he lied.

Maybe the drug didn't work, she thought. She feared for her husband. If the tranquillizer failed him, what would he do?

She put Red's supper on the table and the boy ate quickly.

When the telephone rang, Mrs. O'Malley dashed to it. It was Mayor Frederick.

"Yes, Mayor, the dog gulped down the drugged food. . .Yes, Mayor. Yes. . .Rodney's out now following him, waiting for him to. . .You know, Mayor, it's not Rodney's fault. . .Yes. . .Yes, I'll tell him to call. . ."

While his mother was on the phone Red took the opportunity to grab some food. From the freezer in the basement he took ground moose meat, a moose steak and a whole rabbit. He stuffed the food into a back pack that he used whenever he went fishing, and slipped back to his supper before his mother reentered the kitchen.

"You must have been hungry to eat so fast," she said when she saw Red's plate was empty. She didn't realize he had been down to the basement as well. "Do you want some more?"

"No thanks," he answered, although he was still hungry.

She returned to the living room and kept a lookout through the window. While she was busy, Red hurried around getting the rest of the things he would need — his fishing knife, rags for bandages if Houdini had cuts, and a strip of veneer for splints just in case the dog had broken bones. He also took a book of matches, an axe and a hatchet, an old sauce-pan and a sleeping bag.

While his mother kept watch, Red slipped out the back door, wearing his heavy old parka jacket, and piled everything on his toboggan. He left none too soon, for as he went quietly through the back gate he saw his father coming up the driveway — without Houdini!

Mrs. O'Malley opened the door for her husband. "Where is he?" she asked.

"Got away," he snapped.

"But — he *can't* have got away!" It was not like her to be so excited.

"Beats me how he did it." His voice was subdued, defeated.

Removing his mukluks in the kitchen, he kicked them out of the way and sat down, his shoulders slumped, his head bowed, a beaten man.

"Funny business," he said. "He was drugged all right, running blindly. Got hit by a car, they told me. Boy was seen standing over him. Then both he and the boy disappeared, like a couple o' ghosts."

"A boy?"

"Where's Red?" he asked. "He home yet?"

"Yes, he just had supper. Red?" she called. "Red?"

When Red did not answer she went looking for

him in the annex. He was not there, not in the basement, not in his room. In fact, he was not in the house.

"Rodney," she said, coming back into the kitchen, "he's gone!"

His head snapped up and his face grew stern. "Gone?"

"What's wrong?" Mrs. O'Malley asked. Then she understood. "You mean *Red* could be the boy they saw standing over the dog? Oh, no! He wouldn't do that to his own father."

"I'll skin him alive!" O'Malley roared, jumping up. "He has that dog hidden. Now he's gone to look after him." Furious, he quickly pulled on and laced up his mukluks.

"The Mayor wants you to call him."

"Not now! He can wait. I do the dirty work while he sits at home with his family — while *my* family turns on me!"

He stamped out.

*   *   *

Red hurried along the deserted streets. All the business establishments shut up tight at six o'clock on Christmas Eve and everybody was home. He had no fear of being seen.

He found Houdini still unconscious but breathing. Quickly he pulled him onto the toboggan, strapped him down and set out without losing a second. He headed out of town, dragging his burden behind him.

He needed shelter. It was about twenty below zero. The old trapper's cabin out by the golf course would do for the night.

As the lights dimmed behind him so did the voices of some carollers who were walking through the town, singing in front of houses — singing *Silent Night*.

10
The Search

Leaving the toboggan, Red dug the piled snow away from the doorstep of the trapper's cabin. Finally he swung the door open, bulldozing before it what snow was still left in its way. He pulled the toboggan inside.

Through chinks in the cedar shingles he could see the sky; still, it was shelter. One window had been shattered but he would find some way to block out the cold. The trees that edged the cabin concealed it from the town. It was a perfect place to hide.

From a pocket in his parka Red took a book of matches and scraped one alight. The tiny flame lit the dark cabin long enough for Red to locate the old fireplace and some scrap boards. With light from a second match he set the kindling in place and from another pocket took scrolls of birch bark that he had stripped from a tree on his way to the cabin. When he touched a third match to the birch bark, he had a fire going. The young flame crackled happily and soon shadows began to dance on the wooden walls.

Houdini was still unconscious. By the light that now filled the room Red saw blood on the dog's fur. He removed his mitts and warmed his hands, then unstrapped the dog and lifted him to a blanket on the wooden floor. Like a doctor he examined the dog, talking while he did.

"This won't hurt a bit now, boy. Not a bit. You're going to be all right. Yes, sir, you're going to be fine. No car's going to kill a dog like you. Uh-huh — bad cut on the right shoulder. But the bleeding's stopped. That we can fix. But wait a minute — got to be careful, boy, real careful. . ."

Here he gingerly felt the right paw, pulling it slightly ahead, then pushing it back.

"Broken — yes, I think it's broken. I've never set a broken bone before, Houdini, but it's got to be done. There's nobody else so I'm the one to do it. Lucky you're out cold. What better time? You won't feel a thing."

With that he yanked the paw hard forward and felt the bone snap into place. "There," he said, proud of his skill as a surgeon.

The dog sighed but did not waken.

The fire was growing bigger now, licking higher and higher and shooting sparks upwards. There was the sweet smell of pine burning. The cabin was growing warmer by the minute.

Red got his old saucepan and went outside to fill it with snow. He set it over the fire, then cut bits of splint from the veneer and carefully wrapped the dog's leg. He turned Houdini over on his other side but there were no other wounds, no more broken bones.

When the snow had thawed and the water was warm, he bathed the cut and bandaged it. "There," he said. "It's done."

Red was in no hurry now. He looked around the cabin at the four-poster bed, the old table tumbled on its side, the shelves. The dog was going to be all right as long as he was kept warm. It was cold though, and would grow colder before dawn. The fire must be kept going.

Red began to hack away at the bed and the shelves. They would make dry firewood, more than enough for the night. When he was finished he turned his attention to the broken window. It had to be blocked up to stop all the warm air from rushing outside.

Ripping apart the lumpy old mattress, Red pulled out the grey stuffing and jammed it into the broken window.

Houdini still slept, but it seemed he was dreaming. He was making sounds in his throat. Red unrolled his sleeping bag, removed his boots and crawled into the bag to wait. Houdini would come around.

O'Malley was not the kind of man to tell the town what he feared his son had done. His so-called friends had already laughed at him, humiliated him in a hundred ways, and now his own son had hurt him worse than any of them. He had run off with that dog. Though O'Malley feared what might happen to his only son out there on this frigid winter night, he could not bear to alarm the town, to risk their laughter. Not yet.

But his wife took immediate action. She didn't care what the town thought of the dog, or the dog-catcher. Her son had disappeared into a twenty-below zero night and she was frightened. Quickly she called all the neighbours to find out if they had seen Red. Then she phoned the police.

People began to arrive at the house.

"He wanted a dog," she whispered. "A dog of his own. We should have let him have a dog."

Her friends and neighbours tried to comfort her.

When O'Malley came back from his futile search, he stood in the living room looking through its frosted window and smoking cigarettes. He watched the road, hoping to see Red coming home, but he knew he watched in vain.

The neighbours, seeing him standing alone at the

window, felt sorry for him, and guilty too.

"It's our fault, you know," said one neighbour. "We hounded that dog. He wasn't hurting anyone."

"He's a jinx, though," said another. "There's been nothing but trouble in this town since he came."

"Wait a minute," said a third. "That's nothing to the trouble we've got now. Let's let bygones go by. What we need is to find that boy — and the dog too."

"That's right," said a woman friend of Mrs. O'Malley's. "Christmas can't come for anyone with a lad away from home on a freezing night like this!"

There was a knock at the door and the O'Malleys' minister arrived to offer his sympathy and a prayer for Red's safety. As he prayed, he asked for help for all the lost sheep adrift in the storms this night of the birth of Jesus. Mrs. O'Malley began to cry. O'Malley went over to her and put his hand on her shoulder.

When the minister was finished, Godfrey Aimes spoke up. "Let's get organized. We'll search the whole town."

"Maybe he's hiding out with a friend," a neighbour suggested.

"I called Alty McGregor's house. He wasn't there," said Mrs. O'Malley.

"Surely no parent would hide him, knowing the worry that would cause you," said the minister. "Especially on Christmas Eve, when everyone is at home."

"You're right, Reverend," said O'Malley. "But I'm off to check the streets again."

He was pulling on his mukluks, as were the other men, when Constable Sawchuck from the Ontario Provincial Police arrived. The search party stopped and let him take over. His presence sent hope through everyone in the room, and Mrs. O'Malley dried her eyes and tried to answer his questions.

"What was the boy wearing? When did he leave? What did he take with him?"

Before Officer Sawchuck had gathered all his information, there was a loud knock on the door. When O'Malley flung it open he found Abel Hilkkanen and his brother Veiko standing on the steps.

Abel Hilkkanen was in town for Christmas, staying with his brother who was a bachelor like himself. They had come from Finland together twenty years ago, and every Christmas Eve they got together to reminisce. While they were having a few drinks Veiko told Abel about the runaway boy, son of the dog-catcher, and about the mysterious dog that had caused nothing but trouble since he had come to town.

"A black-and-white dog you say?" asked Abel.

"Yes."

"Average size?" Abel asked.

"Yes," Veiko said.

"By golly, it sounds like Bubba."

"Bubba?" his brother asked.

"Bubba. Old Man Raith's dog. When Raith died last winter that dog just went looney. Wouldn't come to any of us. I guess maybe he came to your town. He followed us out of the bush and to the railway tracks but that's the last we saw of him. That was one smart dog, that Bubba. Come, we'll go see those people, Veiko."

They donned jackets and hauled on their boots. They were both a little tipsy.

When they got to the O'Malley house, Abel all but pushed Constable Sawchuck aside.

"Who's the man of the house?" he asked.

"I am," O'Malley said.

"You got a drink for me and Veiko?"

"You, sir," the police officer said, "have had enough to drink."

Abel shrugged his shoulders. "Okay, okay!"

O'Malley waited silently. Who was this man?

Abel walked to the window and faced the crowd. He acted so self-assured, it seemed he was the one who lived in town and Veiko was the guest. He told the story of Bubba and everyone listened carefully. Nobody doubted the man; he was too confident.

"Mr. O'Malley," he said at last, "tell me about your boy."

"What do you want to know?"

"We know about the dog now, but not about your

boy. He's smart in the woods' like you?" asked Abel.

"Talk to the man, Rodney," his wife urged.

"What kind of boy is your son?" Abel repeated.

"Not much like me," O'Malley muttered, but under the prodding eyes of the others he began to talk.

"He's a loner?"

"Yes," O'Malley said.

"He can take care of himself," Mrs. O'Malley added. "Fish, catch rabbits, ski —"

"Ah," said Abel. "So he *is* like his father. We know he's not with friends."

"Why not?" snapped O'Malley angrily.

" 'Cause he's a loner, that's why. He would not trust anyone to help him," Abel said. "And he knows the woods?"

"Well," O'Malley said.

"He fishes? He hunts? You taught him?"

"No."

"But he likes the outdoors?" Abel went on.

"Yes," answered O'Malley thoughtfully.

Abel turned to Constable Sawchuck.

"Sir, is there a place around he could hole up in? A school building?"

"No," answered the officer. "The schools are too well locked for Red to get in."

"Church?"

The minister quickly dashed that possibility. Every church was going to have a midnight Christmas service and Red would know better.

"That leaves only one other place," cried Abel. "Abandoned buildings. What about abandoned buildings? Any around?"

That led to a babble of information.

"Easy," Abel said, holding up a work-worn hand. "Don't get excited. We'll start from the centre of town and work our way out."

That put some order in the search. It came to light that there was an old fire station, an abandoned garage that once was a car dealership, and a warehouse.

"Good," said Abel. "We got some places to start looking."

"What about the shack at the edge of the golf course?" one man asked.

"Good, good," said Abel. "Every little bit helps. We'll cover all of them. No point all going the same place. We'll split up and come back in an hour. It's a cold one tonight. You get hot coffee back here."

And at last the search for Red got under way.

11
Merry Christmas

The fire sputtered. Red crept out of his sleeping bag to pile on more firewood. The cabin was warm enough.

He checked the dog, but Houdini still slept. Red was tired now but he did not think it would be very smart to go to sleep. When Houdini awoke he might panic. Even if he were not asleep when Houdini recovered from the tranquillizer it was going to be touchy. This dog had always run free. He would see the walls around him, the roof over his head, the fire he was not accustomed to, the boy he did not acknowledge as master or even as friend. Red wondered what the dog would do.

To keep himself awake he decided to eat something. He was hungry, for the hasty supper he had eaten had not done him much good. He thought he would cook some moose burger and put some of it aside for Houdini when he awoke.

He took the meat from his pack and pared off

frozen flakes with his knife. It was hard work and took a long time. Then he set the saucepan over the fire and watched as it began to sizzle. The aroma of frying meat filled the cabin.

Suddenly Houdini's nose twitched. Meat, food, eating. The combination began to bring him back to consciousness.

Stirring the thawing meat in the saucepan with the blade of his knife, Red watched. The dog's nose continued to twitch. His tail moved, but still he slept. Red had begun to eat when Houdini's eyes finally opened.

"Houdini," he said softly, "you're awake." He wanted to pat the dog but he knew that the situation was delicate. He sat back.

The dog's eyes were glassy and depthless.

"Houdini," Red said. "Good boy. You made it."

Houdini lifted his head but could not hold it up. It flopped back. He wanted to stand but his legs were weak. One of them wouldn't do what it should be doing.

He never took his eyes off the boy. He began to snarl, showing his teeth.

Red tried to look unconcerned. He would have to prove that he meant no harm. He threw a piece of the fried meat to Houdini, but the dog didn't look at it.

"Don't blame you," Red said. "That's how he tricked you, isn't it? But I'm your friend, boy. A friend. I'm not going to hurt you. I'm here to take care of you, to see that no one harms you."

He threw wood on the fire. Houdini watched him through blurred eyes, keeping up the growl in his throat.

Red thought of something else. He took the moose steak from his pack and hacked off a chunk of the board-hard meat. Spitting it on his knife, he held it close to the coals. It thawed and began to roast. It smelled good. Houdini watched and sniffed.

When it was done Red held it out to the dog, going closer and closer. Houdini growled louder and tried to pull away from Red. Red stopped. There was no point in rushing and spoiling things. He was satisfied to throw the meat to the dog's mouth. Houdini sniffed it, picked it up slowly, then dropped it again. Suspicious all right, Red thought. Then the dog sniffed it again, picked it up and chewed on it gingerly. He dropped it a second time and sniffed.

"Eat it, boy," Red encouraged. "There's nothing wrong with it. Nothing."

He cut another piece off the steak and roasted it on the coals. Then he began to eat. "See," he said, "I'll eat it too. There's nothing wrong with it. It's good."

At last Houdini ate.

To Red this was victory. He could go to sleep now; the dog had accepted him. He was sleepy too. He took off his parka, and creeping close to Houdini, despite the growls, covered the dog's body with his coat. He wouldn't need it — his sleeping bag would be warm enough. He zipped himself in.

"Go to sleep, boy," he said as he lay down. Houdini watched him beneath half-shut lids until Red's flickering eyelids closed in sleep. They were both sleeping soundly when the search party found them, the boy and the dog, snug in a cabin that cold Christmas Eve.

*   *   *

On Christmas morning the dog was resting peaceful-
ly in the basement and Red was still asleep beside
him. He had fought off all orders to sleep in his own
bed. No, he said. He would sleep in his sleeping bag
right by the dog. He wouldn't leave Houdini un-
protected — not for a moment.

At eight o'clock his father came down the steps to
check on them. He was greeted by a fierce Houdini.
The dog awoke immediately, and lying on his belly,
began to snarl. This noise woke Red, and O'Malley
scurried back up the stairs into the kitchen.

"A man can't even go into his own basement on
account of that dog," he complained.

"Oh, Rodney, be thankful," his wife said.

"My own house," he grumbled.

"We have our son back safe and sound."

"True enough," he answered.

"It's not so much to let him keep the dog," she
said.

"Where am I to stay? In a doghouse? That dog
hates me."

She turned to him. "He has a reason to, dear. But
he'll change. Everything changes. Everybody
changes."

"You can say that again. Look at me! Allowing a
dog into my house. And look at the dog I've
allowed!"

Red entered the kitchen happily. "Morning, Mom.

Morning, Pop. Merry Christmas."

"Merry Christmas, son," Mrs. O'Malley said, hugging the boy.

"Merry Christmas," his father said.

The kitchen was filled with the smell of bacon and eggs.

"Mmmm," Red said. "Smells great."

"I guess you're good and hungry."

"I could eat a horse, Mom," he said. "Me and Houdini."

"Humph," his father said.

Then the telephone rang.

O'Malley picked it off the hook.

"Yes?" he said. Covering the transmitter, he whispered to his wife, "It's Mayor Frederick. Yes, Mayor," he said aloud into the transmitter. "What can I do for you?. . .Yes, we got him."

"In your house?" the Mayor asked.

"In the basement. Guess you heard about my boy?"

"Sure, sure. But the dog, man. What's keeping you? Get rid of it. Put the mutt to sleep."

"No, Mayor. That's what I'm trying to tell you. My boy wants to keep the dog. They've taken to each other. And after all, considering what he went through to save the dog, how can we say no?"

"Say that again," said the Mayor. "I don't think I heard you correctly."

"My boy's keeping the dog, Mayor."

"Poppycock, man. Ridiculous."

"It's Christmas, Mayor."

"A dog-catcher can't take in a stray mongrel like that. You're fired, O'Malley. You hear me? Fired!"

"You can't fire me, Mayor. I quit."

"But —" the Mayor shouted.

"A Merry Christmas to you," O'Malley answered. "Merry Christmas to you and your family." And with that he hung up.

"Did you hear that, Mom?" Red cried. He put his hand on his father's arm, standing closer than the man and boy had stood in years. "Thanks, Pop," he said.

"Merry Christmas," his father said.

The two of them stood together for a while looking through the picture window at the town, quiet now and serene. The town and the hills were Christmas white, and ribbons of white smoke rose from the chimneys and lost themselves in the heavens.

Suddenly there was a tremendous barking from the basement.

"Excuse me, Pop," said Red. "I got to go look after my dog."

*   *   *

They say in the town that O'Malley is a changed man. He and his son Red are closer now. He takes Red to the trapline whenever he can and the boy is fast becoming a skilled woodsman. Even more amazing, they say that O'Malley has taken to the dog and the dog to him. He takes Houdini along with him when he goes into the woods. He says the dog can spot a grouse at five hundred paces and earns every cent of his keep with the rabbits he flushes out of the underbrush.

But there are those who say that O'Malley just plain likes the dog. Who can tell? One thing is sure, if Red is out of school and it's time to go out to the bush to check the trapline — all three of them go together.